This Little Pig

A Mother Goose Favorite

LEONARD B. LUBIN

LOTHROP, LEE & SHEPARD BOOKS
NEW YORK

For
Daniel Halioua
and
Ruby Sheets

First Edition. 1 2 3 4 5 6 7 8 9 10

LIBRARY OF CONGRESS CATALOGING IN PUBLICATION DATA.

Main entry under title: This little pig. Summary: The nursery rhyme beginning "This little pig went to market" is illustrated with eighteenth-century pigs who enact the tale with extravagant embellishment. 1. Nursery rhymes. 2. Children's poetry. [1. Nursery rhymes] I. Lubin, Leonard B., ill. PZ8.3.T293 1985 398'.8 84-10021 ISBN 0-688-04088-8 ISBN 0-688-04089-6 (lib. bdg.)

This
little pig
went
to market,

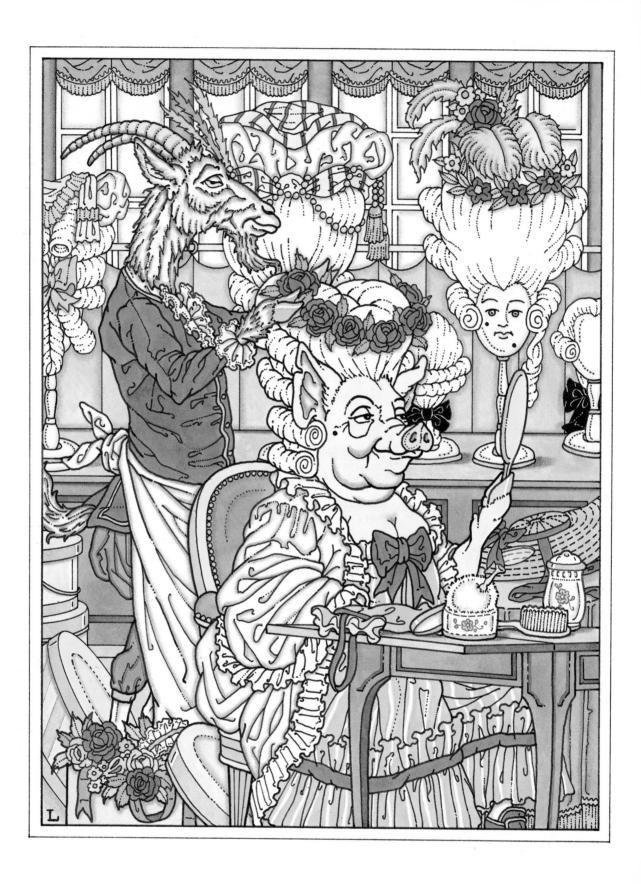

This
little pig
stayed home,

This
little pig
had
roast beef,

This
little pig
had none,

And this little pig
cried,
Wee-wee-wee,
All the way
home.